Little Man's Misadventures

Little Man's Misadventures

by
M. SAVERIO CLEMENTE

Illustrations by
R. L. CLEMENTE

RESOURCE *Publications* · Eugene, Oregon

LITTLE MAN'S MISADVENTURES

Resource Publications
An Imprint of Wipf and Stock Publishers
199 W. 8th Ave., Suite 3
Eugene, OR 97401

www.wipfandstock.com

PAPERBACK ISBN: 978-1-5326-5230-1
HARDCOVER ISBN: 978-1-5326-5231-8
EBOOK ISBN: 978-1-5326-5232-5

Manufactured in the U.S.A.   08/17/18

In Memory of the Aunts and Uncle Ray
who instilled in us a love of reading, writing, drawing,
and learning.

Life is a great adventure. Everywhere you go, there's something unexpected just waiting to happen.

~ Little Man's crazy uncle

Contents

story one

Clumsy Little Man

or

Life is an Adventure

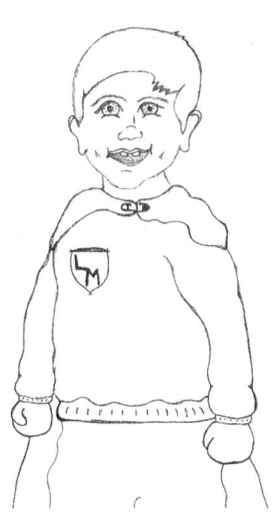

Everyone who knows Little Man knows that he is clumsy. He is always bumping into walls, stepping on toys, tripping over his own feet, and knocking things on the floor. Sometimes he even slips on nothing at all and falls right down on his butt.

One day when he was walking through the cafeteria at school, he tripped over his shoelaces and spilled an entire tray of lasagna in Principle Grumpton's lap. Little Man said that it was an accident but that didn't save him from having detention for a whole week.

When he went to his friend's house, he couldn't reach the doorbell. He leaned over the railing to try to ring it and ended up falling off the porch into a big green bush. When his friend's mom came to the door, she looked around but she did not see him.

"Down here!" Little Man said.

"What are you doing in that bush?" his friend's mom said.

"I'm stuck," Little Man said.

"Were you trying to hide from me?" his friend's mom said.

"No," Little Man said. "I rang the bell and fell in."

"So," his friend's mom said, "you like to play dingdong ditch, do you?"

"No," Little Man said. "I can't get out!"

She left him there and called his parents. And when they heard that he was trying to play a dirty trick, they made him go to bed without any dessert.

Last Christmas, Little Man wanted to be the one to put the star on top of the Christmas tree.

"I don't think it's a good idea, Little Man," his father said.

"I can do it," Little Man said.

"Are you sure?" his father said.

"I know I can," Little Man said.

He carefully removed the star from the box and plugged it into the outlet behind the tree. It glimmered and shined with light. Then he slowly climbed up onto the stepstool.

"Careful, Little Man," his father said.

"I'm always careful," Little Man said.

He got to the top step and reached for the highest branch.

"It might be too high," his father said.

Little Man stepped up on his tiptoes.

"I'm not sure you can reach it," his father said.

Little Man extended both of his arms.

"Oh no!" his father said.

Suddenly, Little Man lost his balance and began frantically swinging from side to side.

"Watch out!" his father yelled.

Crash! Little Man fell forward into the tree and pulled the entire thing to the ground. Ornaments and Christmas lights and pine needles went flying everywhere.

Meow! The tree startled the cat. She let out an awful screech and jumped up into Little Man's father's arms.

"Ouch!" his father said.

The cat was so scared that she clawed his face. Then she jumped down out of his arms and hid under a chair.

"Sorry," Little Man said as he climbed out of the tree.

"Are you ok?" his father said.

"I'm ok," Little Man said and he brushed the pine needles out of his hair.

"Good," his father said. "Now go to your room while I clean up this mess."

"But it was an accident," Little Man said.

"Go," his father said and he pointed to the stairs.

"Ok," Little Man said with a frown.

He walked to the stairs and began to climb up to his bedroom.

"Little Man," his father said.

"Yes?" Little Man said.

(He was hoping that his father would ask him to help clean up).

"This is the last time I'm going to let you decorate the top of the tree," his father said.

Little Man went to his room and sat on the end of his bed.

The cat came up a short time later but when Little Man leaned over to pet her, he sneezed and she ran out meowing.

That night, it was snowing outside and Little Man's crazy uncle came over for dinner. I call him Little Man's "crazy" uncle because he was not like most people. Whereas everyone else seemed sick and tired of Little Man's clumsy ways, his crazy uncle saw things differently.

"Being clumsy," he said, "doesn't have to be a curse. In fact, I think it's one of the best things about you."

"How could being clumsy be a good thing?" Little Man said.

"What is the clumsiest thing you've ever done?" his crazy uncle said.

"I don't know," Little Man said. "Maybe the time I crashed my bicycle into Mrs. Krankster's parked car."

"Did you get hurt?" his crazy uncle said.

"No," he said. "Not really."

"Did anyone see you?" his crazy uncle said.

"Yes," Little Man said. "Some of the neighborhood kids."

"What did they do?" his crazy uncle said.

"They laughed," Little Man said.

"And what did Mrs. Krankster do?" his crazy uncle said.

"She scrunched up her face real tight until she looked just like her yappy little dog. Then she turned as red as a tomato and yelled, 'What did you do to my car you little monster?!'"

His crazy uncle laughed at his impersonation of the crotchety old lady.

"I guess it was kind of funny," Little Man said.

"Listen, Little Man," his crazy uncle said, "there are things in life that you should take seriously, but taking yourself *too seriously* means pretending to be someone you're not. Everyone makes mistakes. Everyone does silly, strange, ridiculous things. That's what it is be human. And being able to laugh at those things means being able to recognize that sometimes you aren't perfect. Sometimes you're a little crazy."

"Or a little clumsy," Little Man said.

"Or a lot clumsy," his crazy uncle said.

Little Man laughed.

"If we didn't do such funny things," his crazy uncle said, "life wouldn't be as interesting."

"Sometimes I wish life was a little less interesting," Little Man said.

"No," his crazy uncle said. "Life is a great adventure. Everywhere you go, there's something unexpected just waiting to happen."

"But it seems like I'm always the one causing unexpected things to happen," Little Man said.

"That's true," his crazy uncle said. "But that just means that your adventures are *misadventures*. The funniest thing about the trouble you get into is that it surprises even you!"

"I never try to do clumsy things," Little Man said. "They just seem to happen."

"If you can learn to laugh at the silly stuff you do," his crazy uncle said, "you won't feel so embarrassed. You may even realize that there's something good about things not going right. Sometimes things going wrong can be good too."

"That's a funny way to look at things," Little Man said.

"I know it sounds crazy," his crazy uncle said. "But trust me. It works."

After dinner, Little Man got up to do the dishes.

"Not tonight," his father said. "I don't want a repeat of the mess you made earlier."

"I can do it!" Little Man said.

His face turned red.

"Why don't you get your jacket," his crazy uncle said. "We'll let your mom and dad handle the dishes and we can go sledding before the sun goes down."

"Can I, mom?" Little Man said. "Can I, dad?"

"Go ahead," his mother said. "Just make sure you wear your hat and mittens."

Little Man raced to the closet, threw on his jacket and his hat and mittens, and ran out the door.

"Come on, uncle!" he yelled. "Before it gets dark!"

"Wait, Little Man!" his crazy uncle called after him. "You forgot your—"

When Little Man's feet hit the cold, wet snow, he realized that in his excitement he had forgotten to put on his boots. His socks were soaked all the way through and his toes were numb. His crazy uncle stood in the doorway, holding up his boots and laughing. Then he took off his own shoes and ran barefoot into the yard.

"What are you doing?" Little Man said.

"Quick!" his crazy uncle said. "The faster you run, the less you notice how cold your feet are!"

He chased Little Man around the yard and the two laughed and played until the sun set in the winter sky.

story two

Christmas Eve at Nana and Papa's

or

Timing is Everything

IT WAS THE MORNING of Christmas Eve and Little Man's mother was in the kitchen. She was standing in front of the stove stirring a wood spoon around and around in a big metal pot.

"What are you doing?" Little Man said.

"I'm making mushroom soup," his mother said.

"We learned at school that mushrooms are a type of fungus," Little Man said.

"That's true," his mother said.

"Gross!" Little Man said. "I don't want to eat fungus soup."

His mother laughed.

"It's yummy," she said. "My uncle used to go and pick wild mushrooms in the forest and he would make Hungarian mushroom soup every Christmas Eve. I have his old family recipe and now I make the soup. It's a Christmas tradition."

"Did you pick those mushrooms yourself?" Little Man said.

"No," his mother said. "I wouldn't even know where to look."

"I want to pick wild mushrooms," Little Man said.

"But you just said that mushrooms are gross," his mother said.

"That's ok," Little Man said. "I like gross things. One time I saw a toad in the woods and I thought it was dead because it wasn't moving. But then my friend Conor dared me to touch it and I wanted to be brave so I picked up a long, knotted stick and I poked it."

"Then what happened?" his mother said.

"Then it started jumping and croaking and it landed right on Conor's shoe!"

"What did he do?" his mother said.

"He went running home and threw his shoes in the trash. But his dad found them the next day and took them out of the trash and he still has to wear them—even though they have toad juice on them!"

His mother laughed.

"And one time," Little Man said, "Justin found a wad of gum stuck under the table at lunch and it was old and hard and had been there for years. He scraped it off and showed us and he said it felt more like a rock than like gum. Then Ryan bet me his dessert that I wouldn't chew it. I told him I wouldn't chew it but I would put it in my mouth for five whole seconds if he gave me the rest of his chocolate milk. He said that that was a good deal and we shook on it. I was just about to put it in my mouth when Principle Grumpton came over. He asked me what I was doing and I had to show him the gum. He made me throw it away and he sent us out to recess and I never got that chocolate milk."

His mother cringed and held her belly.

"What's wrong?" Little Man said.

"Nothing," his mother said. "Just a cramp."

"Are you ok?" Little Man said.

"Yes," his mother said. "I'm ok."

She smiled.

Little Man looked at her belly. It was big and round and it looked like she was hiding a beach ball under her sweater. Little Man knew that his mother had a baby inside of her and that soon she would give birth to a little boy, a brother for Little Man to play with and protect.

"Come here, Little Man," his mother said. "The baby is kicking."

Little Man walked over and put his hand on his mother's belly. Then something amazing happened. Somewhere deep inside of her, Little Man's little brother was pushing his foot out, stretching and kicking and extending his tiny baby leg.

Little Man laughed.

"When can I meet him?" he said.

"Soon," his mother said. "He's going to be here soon."

Little Man leaned in and kissed his mother's belly. Then he cupped his hands and pressed them against her stomach and whispered something that his mother could not hear.

She smiled and rubbed his hair.

Little Man had seen his father bend down and talk to his mother's belly many times before. The first time he saw it, he thought it was pretty silly.

"What are you doing?" he said.

"I'm talking to the baby so that he knows the sound of my voice," his father said.

"Can the baby really hear you talk?" Little Man said.

"Yes," his father said. "I used to talk to you like this too."

"What do you mean?" Little Man said.

"When you were inside of your mother's belly," his father said, "I used to lean in and whisper to you. Sometimes I'd even sing."

"I was in there?!" Little Man said.

It was a strange thought. But his father insisted that it was true.

Later that day, when Little Man was outside playing in the snow, he heard his father calling to him from the doorway.

"Little Man," his father said. "Nana and Papa are going to pick you up and you're going to stay with them tonight. Your mother is ready to have the baby."

"Tonight?" Little Man said. "But it's Christmas Eve!"

"I know," his father said. "You'll spend Christmas Eve at Nana and Papa's house and hopefully I'll be able to pick you up tomorrow morning."

"Can't the baby wait?" Little Man said. "Can't he come in a couple of days instead?"

"No," his father said. "He's coming tonight."

Little Man was worried. What if Santa didn't know that he was sleeping over Nana and Papa's house? What if he couldn't figure out where to leave the presents?

Little Man's Nana and Papa came over a short time later and his mother and father left for the hospital.

"What's wrong, Little Man?" Nana said. "Aren't you excited to be a big brother?"

"It's Christmas Eve, Nana," Little Man said. "How will Santa know that I'm staying at your house?"

"Santa knows," Nana said. "Santa always knows."

It was a little after seven o'clock and Little Man was already in his pajamas. He was sitting by the fireplace, drinking hot cocoa, and listening to Nana read aloud from *A Christmas Carol* by Charles Dickens. She had just started the second chapter—the part where the first of the three spirits visits Scrooge. The fire in the fireplace was crackling and warm.

The phone rang in the kitchen and Papa got up to answer it.

"Keep reading, Nana," Little Man said.

"'The spirit wore a tunic of the purest white,'" Nana read. "'And round its waist was bound a lustrous belt, the sheen of which was beautiful.'"

"Get your coats," Papa called from the kitchen. "The new baby is here. We're going to the hospital to meet him."

Little Man jumped up and ran to the closet. He put on his coat and his hat and gloves.

"Don't forget your boots," Nana said. "I heard about what happened when your uncle came to visit."

"I won't forget," Little Man said and he pulled his boots on over his footie pajamas.

It was snowing outside and Little Man sat in the backseat of Papa's truck, bundled up in his puffy winter jacket. He looked out the window and watched the snow fall soft and white, dusting the earth like powder on his favorite kind of donut. The radio was on and Papa was singing along to *Dominic the Donkey*, Little Man's favorite Christmas song.

When they got to the hospital, they parked in the parking garage and took the elevator up to the main lobby. Papa walked over to a receptionist sitting behind a big, wooden desk and asked how to get to the maternity ward.

"What's a maternity ward?" Little Man said.

"That's the floor of the hospital where babies are born," Nana said.

The receptionist told them that they had to get back into the elevator and take it to the third floor. They got in and, as the doors began to close, something caught Little Man's eye. Walking through the lobby in a red jacket and black boots was a fat, jolly, red-cheeked Santa Claus.

Little Man didn't have time to think. He had to act.

He ran out of the elevator and the doors closed shut behind him.

"Little Man!" Papa called.

But it was too late. The elevator was already on its way up to the third floor and Little Man was left standing alone in the lobby.

Nana and Papa were worried. The moment the elevator reached the third floor, Papa ran out, found the stairs, and began descending them as fast as he could. (He was running so fast that he almost tripped). Nana stayed in the elevator and rode it back down to the ground floor. But when she got there, Little Man was gone.

Papa came running over.

"Where is he?" he said.

He was out of breath.

"I don't know," Nana said. "We have to find him. Quick!"

They went from room to room, peeking their heads in to see if Little Man had wandered in by mistake. After a few minutes of looking, they notified the hospital police who helped them continue their search. An announcement was made over the loud speakers and everyone was made aware: Little Man was missing and needed to be found right away.

After half an hour, they became very worried. Where could Little Man be? What if he was hurt or in trouble?

"Here he is!" Nana cried. "I found him! I found him!"

Everyone came running. They were so relieved.

Little Man had followed Santa through the hospital. He had wanted to tell him that he was spending the night at Nana and Papa's house and that Santa should leave his presents there. But Santa had turned a corner and disappeared. When Little Man turned the same corner, he didn't see Santa anywhere. Instead, he found a woman sitting in a chair outside of one of the hospital rooms. Her face was buried in her hands. She was crying.

Little Man sat down in the chair next to her.

She didn't seem to notice.

He put his hand on her lap.

She continued to cry.

He sat there and didn't say anything.

After about a half an hour, he saw Nana walking down the other end of the hall. He got up from his chair and walked over to see her.

The woman stood up, dried her eyes, and went back into the hospital room.

"Nana," Little Man called.

Nana turned.

"Oh, thank God," she said and she dropped down on her knees and hugged him tight.

She began kissing him all over and squeezed him and squeezed him until he couldn't breathe.

"Here he is!" she called. "I found him! I found him!"

After the commotion had died down, they walked back to the elevators.

This time, Papa made sure that Little Man was holding his hand.

"We were very worried," Papa said in a stern voice.

"I'm sorry, Papa," Little Man said. "I just wanted to see Santa Claus."

They got into the elevator and took it up to the third floor.

The elevator dinged as the doors opened.

They walked down the hall of the maternity ward.

"We'll have to be very quiet when we enter the room," Nana said. "We don't want to scare the new baby."

As they turned the corner, Little Man saw a group of people wearing Christmas sweaters gathered together outside of his mother's room. They were walking door to door, singing carols for those spending their holiday in the hospital.

One of them handed Little Man a candy cane.

He smiled and said thank you.

The carolers moved away from the door so that Nana and Papa and Little Man could enter. And waiting inside were his mother and father and the new baby who was fast asleep in the arms of a fat, jolly, red-faced Santa Claus. Everyone was laughing and singing and Little Man's mother was so happy that she began to cry.

story three

Little Monster

or

Big Things Come in Small Packages

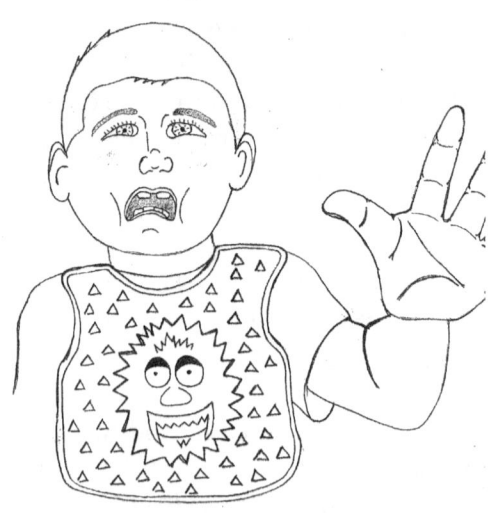

LITTLE MAN'S MOTHER AND baby brother had to spend Christmas and the day after Christmas in the hospital. Little Man opened his presents at Nana and Papa's house and then his father met the three of them at church for mass. It was an old stone church with high stained glass windows and a green carpet that was tattered from years of use. The altar was decorated with red and white roses, tall poinsettias and snow-white lilies. There was a life size manger in the back by the vestibule and there was a white star hanging above it that glimmered and shined with light.

"Look, Little Man," Nana said. "The baby in the manger looks like your new brother."

"I wish my brother was born in a manger," Little Man said.

"Why's that?" Nana said.

"Because then I would get to play with the animals."

"Don't you remember the petting zoo?" Nana said. "How the lamb sneezed and it startled you and you fell right in the mud?"

"I remember," Little Man said. "But there's no mud in a manger."

"No," his father said. "Only hay."

"What's wrong with hay?" Little Man said.

"You're allergic to hay," his father said.

"That's ok," Little Man said. "I'd bring plenty of tissues."

After mass, Little Man and his family went to the hospital to spend the afternoon with his mother and the new baby. When he wasn't sleeping, the baby would scrunch up his face and yawn or make soft cooing sounds with his tiny, toothless mouth. Little Man asked if he could hold him in his arms but his father said that he didn't think it was a good idea.

"He's very small, Little Man. I don't want you to drop him."

"I won't drop him!" Little Man said. "I never drop anything!"

And to show how upset he was, he banged his fist on the nightstand.

Sitting on the nightstand was a glass of orange juice and when Little Man banged his fist, the glass fell to the floor.

Crash! Juice spilled everywhere.

"What a mess!" Papa said.

"I'm sorry," Little Man said. "It was an accident."

"Come here, Little Man," his mother said. "Maybe your father will feel more comfortable with you holding the baby if you sit next to me on the bed and we surround you with pillows."

"Can I, dad?" Little Man said.

"I don't know . . ." his father said.

"Please?" Little Man said.

"You can," his mother said. "But first, get some napkins and clean up that juice."

When Little Man was done sopping up the sticky mess, he climbed onto the bed and positioned himself in the crook of his mother's arm.

"The baby, please," he said.

His father looked uneasy.

"You have to be very careful," his mother said.

"I'm always careful," Little Man said.

"That's what I'm afraid of," his father said.

Nevertheless, he surrounded Little Man with big, fluffy pillows and then gently placed the baby into his arms.

"Hi," Little Man said as he looked down into the baby's big blue eyes. "I'm your brother. We're going to be friends. If you cry, I will get you something to eat. If you stink, I will tell mom to change your diaper. If you're cold, I'll get you a blanket. If you're hot, I'll turn on the fan. And if you want a toy, you can have one—as long as I'm not already playing with it."

The baby cooed and Little Man giggled.

"Hi," he said. "I'm going to teach you to play football and to build snow forts. I'll show you how to climb trees and I'll let you help me look for salamanders under the rocks in the backyard. When you get bigger, we'll ride the bus together. And we can trade baseball cards and ride bicycles and make our own war movies using dad's old camera."

The baby stretched out his little baby arm and reached up with his little baby hand and wrapped his fingers right around Little Man's nose.

"Hey!" Little Man said. "Let go!"

But the baby didn't let go. He squeezed with all his baby might.

"Ah!" Little Man yelled. "Get off!"

The baby was pulling on his nose and giggling and even though Little Man was turning his head from side to side, he could not break free from the baby's grasp.

"Let go!" Little Man cried. "You're pulling my nose off!"

It was a squeezing, wrenching, grasping, clutching grip.

The baby was much stronger than anyone would have guessed. He was stronger than anyone thought a little baby could be.

"Help!" Little Man said. "Someone help!"

"Ok, Little Man," his father said. "Settle down. I'll take him from you now."

He walked over and took the baby from Little Man's arms. But still the baby would not let go.

"Nana," his father said. "Can you give us a hand?"

Nana came over and tried to pry the baby's fingers from Little Man's nose. But *still* the baby would not let go.

"Papa," she said. "We need your help."

But Papa was just as unsuccessful as the others. The baby's grip was too tight. It could not be broken.

"I'm going to lose my nose!" Little Man said. "He's going to pull it right off of my face!"

Little Man's mother leaned in and began tugging on the baby's arm, pulling it this way and that way. Finally, she was able to loosen his clenched fist and free Little Man from his tiny grasp. The baby began crying frantically and reaching back toward his brother's face. He was trying to grab hold of the nose once more.

"Get away!" Little Man cried. "Get away, little monster!"

"It's ok," his mother said. "You'll both be alright."

"Don't let him grab me!" Little Man said.

"It's ok," his mother said. "It's alright."

After a few minutes, everyone settled down. The baby stopped crying and fell fast asleep and Little Man's nose turned from bright red back to its normal color.

"I think we're going to have our hands full with this one," Little Man's father said.

"He had his hands full of my nose!" Little Man said.

Everyone started laughing—even Little Man.

"I guess it was kind of funny," he said. "Or at least it's funny now that he let go."

"Who knew a baby could grip so tight?" Papa said.

"That's no baby," Nana said. "That's our Little Monster. His big brother gave him his first nickname."

"Yes," Little Man's father said. "Now we have a Little Man *and* a Little Monster. The house is getting crowded."

"It's not too crowded," Little Man said. "There's still room for one more."

"What do you mean?" his mother said. "I don't think we're going to have a third baby any time soon."

"Not another baby," Little Man said. "A puppy."

"A puppy?" his father said. "We don't have room for a puppy. Where would he sleep?"

"He could sleep in the baby's room," Little Man said, "and Little Monster could sleep in his crate—that way he won't be able to pull my nose in the middle of the night."

"Little Monster's not sleeping in a crate!" his mother said.

"Please," Little Man said.

"If you want a puppy," his father said, "you're going to have to show us you can care for one."

"But how can I do that?" Little Man said.

"You can start by helping out more around the house. You're a big brother now. That means that your little brother is going to look up to you and depend on you. And we will be depending on you too."

"I'm ready to be a big brother," Little Man said. "And I'll be an extra good one if it means I can have a puppy."

"I know you will," his father said. "I have no doubt about that."

story four

Pizza Again?

or

Promise Not to Tell

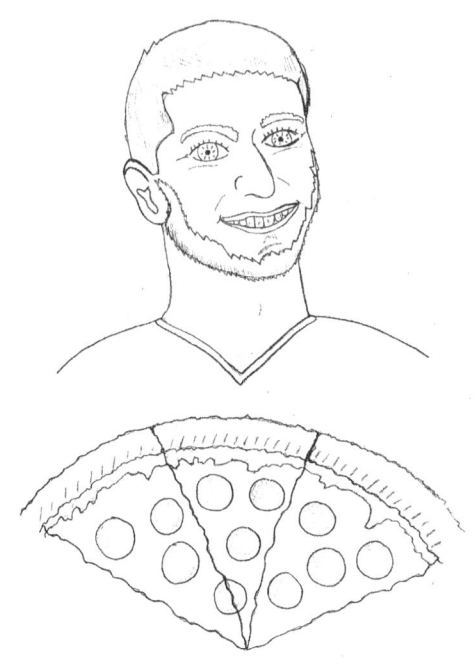

IF LITTLE MAN'S MOTHER knew that while she and Little Monster were in the hospital, Little Man and his father were eating nothing but pizza, she would have been very upset. After all, she always made healthy meals that tasted good too. But if Little Man was being honest, his mother's meals didn't taste as good as pizza—nothing did. Pizza was Little Man's favorite food and he wanted to eat it for breakfast, lunch, and dinner.

After leaving the hospital on Christmas night, Little Man and his father ordered their dinner from *Charlie's Pizzeria*—the only place open on Christmas—and they ate it in front of the TV (something Little Man's mother never let them do). Little Man was so tired from all of the excitement of the day that he fell asleep halfway through *The Muppets Christmas Carol* and his father had to carry him to bed on his shoulder. The next morning, the two of them ate cold pizza for breakfast and they washed it down with chocolate milk.

"Mom never lets me drink chocolate milk before lunchtime," Little Man said.

"Well," his father said, "your mother's not here. We'll keep it our secret."

Little Man smiled.

"I promise not to tell," he said.

"Good," his father said. "I won't tell her either. It'll stay just between us."

"She should have babies more often," Little Man said.

"Careful what you wish for, Little Man," his father said. "This house will get awfully crowded."

"That's ok," Little Man said. "I like babies. And besides, I can help you take care of them. I'm the big brother."

"That's good," his father said, "because we're going to need your help. Babies are a lot of work."

"Was I a lot of work?" Little Man said.

"You still are," his father said.

"Hey!" Little Man said.

His father laughed.

"I'm only kidding," he said. "You were a good baby. And now you're my good little man."

Little Man smiled.

"Someday," he said, "I'm going to be a big man. And when I am, I'll eat pizza for every meal and drink nothing but chocolate milk."

"Being a big man means more than doing whatever you want to do," his father said. "A lot of times it means giving up what you want for the sake of someone else."

"Like giving my chocolate milk to my little brother?" Little Man said.

His father smiled.

"Something like that," he said.

"I don't think I'm ready to be a big man," Little Man said. "At least not yet."

"Good," his father said. "I don't think I'm ready for you to be a big man either."

At lunchtime, his father asked him what he wanted to eat and Little Man replied that he wanted pizza and chocolate milk.

"Again?" his father said.

"It was *so* good," Little Man said. "Just one more time. Just one."

"Ok," his father said. "But this really needs to be our secret."

Little Man promised and he enjoyed every bite.

When it was time for dinner, Little Man's father realized that there was no food in the pantry and that they would need to go grocery shopping before he could make a meal.

"Can't we just order *Charlie's*?" Little Man said.

"Pizza again?" his father said. "No. Enough is enough. We need to eat a real dinner. Something healthy."

"But pizza is healthy," Little Man said. "The tomato sauce counts as a vegetable and the cheese has lots of calcium for my bones. And if you order a bacon, pineapple pizza, we can get some protein and some fruit too. What's healthier than that?"

"I don't think so," his father said. "I'll pick up some chicken and veggies and make us a stir fry."

"But I'm hungry now," Little Man said. "Groceries will take too long. If you order *Charlie's*, it will be ready by the time we pick it up."

His father rubbed his chin as if he was thinking long and hard about what to do.

Then his stomach made a loud grumbling noise like an old man snoring and he said, "Ok, but this is the last time. No more pizza after tonight."

"Yay!" Little Man said. "And I want chocolate milk to go with it."

They picked up the pizza and on the way home, Little Man's father drove the car down a side street that Little Man did not recognize.

"Where are we going?" Little Man said.

"You'll see," his father said.

The street was dark and quiet and no one was outside.

They turned down another street and another and soon Little Man saw the bright glow of Christmas lights.

"What's that?" Little Man said.

"That's the Fatima Shrine," his father said. "Every year at Christmas time, it's decorated with lights and ornaments and all of the trees are lit up. There's music and singing and cider and cocoa."

"Wow," Little Man said. "It's like a million colored stars, tiny and burning bright."

"It's pretty good," his father said.

"Good?" Little Man said. "It's beautiful. I've never seen so many lights."

"I know," his father said. "They do a great job decorating."

Little Man and his father sat and ate their pizza in the car; and even though it was so cold that they could see their breath, they rolled down their windows so they could listen to the music coming from the Shrine.

"Christmas was yesterday," Little Man said. "Why haven't they taken the lights down?"

"Christmas doesn't end on Christmas Day," his father said.

"It doesn't?" Little Man said.

"No," his father said. "Christmas Day is just the beginning. There are twelve days of Christmas and then the Christmas season doesn't officially end until February 2nd. We have a lot more celebrating to do."

"I'm glad that we're celebrating with pizza," Little Man said.

"Me too," his father said. "And when we're done eating, we can buy some cocoa and walk around the Shrine."

The next morning, Little Man woke up early, before his father was out of bed. He was very quiet and tiptoed down the stairs so as not to make a sound. Then he opened the refrigerator, pulled out the box of pizza from the night before, and looked inside.

There were still four slices left.

"Jackpot!" Little Man said.

"What do you think you're doing?"

Little Man turned quickly and saw his father watching him from the doorway.

"Oh," Little Man said. "I was . . ."

"You better not eat that pizza," his father said. "Not without sharing a slice with me."

Little Man smiled.

"Your mother will be home this afternoon," his father said. "Let's make sure we finish all of the pizza before then and I'll get rid of the boxes."

"Deal," Little Man said. "And I won't say a word."

"Promise?" his father said.

"Promise," Little Man said. "I'll never tell."

story five

The Lost Donut

or

Sharing is Caring

LITTLE MAN'S LITTLE BROTHER was very little. For the first few months of his life, he was too little to play, too little to talk, too little to do much of anything except cry and sleep and poop. Sometimes he cried because he needed to sleep. Sometimes he cried because he had just pooped. And sometimes he cried because he wanted to cry or for no reason at all. He was too little to stand or sit up on his own and he couldn't even roll himself onto his belly. He slept in a blue basinet in Little Man's parent's bedroom and he cried and yelled all night, waking everyone in the house and keeping them awake until morning.

"Why does he cry so much?" Little Man asked one afternoon.

His mother was trying to rock the baby back to sleep.

"Well," she said, "crying is a baby's way of communicating. He cries in order to tell us that he needs something."

"I wish he'd find another way of communicating," Little Man said. "Like whispering."

"Shhh," his mother said. "I think he's almost asleep."

She gently laid the baby in his basinet and began to tiptoe out of the room.

Little Man followed, trying hard not to make a sound. But as he walked through the doorway, he tripped over the edge of the carpet and—THUD!—bumped his head right on the wall.

"Ouch!" he said.

"Waaaaah!" The baby woke up and started screaming at the top of his lungs.

"Not again!" Little Man said.

He rolled his eyes.

"Come here, Little Man," his mother said.

She kissed his forehead.

"Now," she said, "go over and let your brother hold your hand. Sometimes babies just need to be comforted. Sometimes they need to know that they're not alone."

Little Man walked over and put his finger in the palm of his baby brother's tiny hand.

"It's ok, Little Monster," he said. "I'm here. You're alright."

The baby settled down and soon he stopped crying altogether.

"It's working," Little Man said.

The baby cooed.

"I think he likes me," Little Man said.

"I think he does," his mother said.

Then Little Monster took Little Man's finger and put it right in his mouth.

"Eww!" Little Man said. "Cut it out!"

He pulled his finger away.

When he did, the baby burst into tears.

"Little Man," his mother said. "He's just a baby."

"He's getting his baby slobber all over me!" Little Man said.

His mother took the baby out of the basinet and began rocking him in her arms. She whispered to him and sang to him in a soft, soothing voice.

"It's not fair," Little Man said. "All he does is cry. He doesn't want to play or draw or do anything fun."

"Someday," his mother said, "the two of you will be best friends."

"I don't know," Little Man said. "Not if he keeps acting like this."

"Someday," his mother said, "you'll be inseparable."

"I hope so," Little Man said. "I don't want a baby brother forever. I want a brother-brother to play with and protect."

"And that's just what you'll have," his mother said. "But until then, you can always play with your cousin Cora. She's like a sister, only better."

"Why better?" Little Man said.

"Because whenever she comes over," his mother said, "she makes Auntie buy you donuts for lunch."

"Mmm," Little Man said. "I love donuts."

His mouth began to water.

"Why don't I call Auntie?" his mother said. "I can ask if she wants to bring Cora by this afternoon for a playdate."

"Can we have donuts too?" Little Man said.

"I don't know," his mother said. "How about broccoli stew?"

"No," Little Man said. "Donuts."

"What about liver and onions?"

"No," Little Man said. "Donuts."

"How about tofu and lima beans?"

"No fooling," Little Man said. "I want donuts!"

"Ok," his mother said. "I'll mention that too. Now go outside and play in the yard. I'll rock Little Monster back to sleep and then I'll call Auntie and ask her about coming over."

Little Man loved playing outside. It was springtime now. The snow had melted, the ice had thawed, and little green buds were beginning to sprout on the trees. There were fat purple worms wriggling around whenever he lifted up rocks and birds jumped from tree to tree, singing and squawking and filling the air with noise. The sun was warm but the air was cool and the grass was damp beneath his feet. Little Man searched the yard for rocks, pretending he was an archeologist hunting for rare dinosaur bones. He collected large sticks and branches and used them to build a secret fort near a clearing in the woods. He discovered an ant hole, covered it with dirt, and watched as the tiny black critters tunneled their way out again. He climbed to the top of an old oak tree and looked out over the yard, pretending he was a pirate looking out at the ocean from the crow's nest on the mast of a ship.

"*Thar she blows!*" he yelled as his Auntie's car pulled into the driveway.

When it had parked, his Auntie got out, walked around, opened the back the door, and let his cousin Cora out into the yard.

"Cora!" Little Man yelled.

Cora looked around not knowing where he was.

"Up here," Little Man yelled. "I'm a bird making a nest in this tree."

He flapped his arms up and down and waved them back and forth.

"Be careful," his Auntie said. "That's too high!"

"I'm always careful," Little Man said. And as he spoke, he felt himself losing his balance.

"Oh no!" Cora yelled. "Don't fall."

"Oh no!" Little Man yelled. "I'm falling!"

As he plummeted from the tree, Little Man reached out and grabbed ahold of a branch.

"Hang on, Little Man," Cora yelled. "I'm coming!"

"I'm hanging on," Little Man yelled. "Come quick!"

He was dangling about ten feet off the ground when a fat, brown caterpillar crawled from the branch onto his hand and began to tickle his knuckles.

"Eek!" Little Man yelled. "It's so fuzzy!"

Cora ran over as fast as she could but she was too late.

Thump! Little Man fell from the tree to the ground. He landed right on his butt.

"Are you ok?" Cora said.

Little Man was slow to get up.

"Say you're ok," Cora said.

"I'm ok," Little Man said. "Did you bring the donuts?"

Little Man's Auntie came running over.

"What were you thinking?" she said. "You know not to climb that high!"

"I was pretending to be a pirate," Little Man said.

"Hasn't your father warned you about climbing that tree?" his Auntie said.

"He has," Little Man said. "But he's not home. Please don't tell him."

"Ok," his Auntie said. "But promise me you won't climb up there again."

"I promise," Little Man said.

"Good," his Auntie said. "Then this will stay between us."

Little Man and Cora spent the afternoon playing in the yard. They rode their bikes in the driveway and took turns pushing each other in the wagon. They drew on the sidewalk with chalk and collected bugs in a big glass jar. They played catch with the football and Cora showed Little Man some of the dance moves she had been practicing for her upcoming recital. They were having so much fun that they almost forgot about lunch. Then Little Man's stomach began to grumble.

"What was that?" Cora said.

"That was my belly," Little Man said. "I'm getting hungry."

"I thought that was a roaring tiger!" Cora said.

They both laughed.

When they entered the house, they found Little Man's mother and his Auntie sitting at the kitchen table. They were sipping tea and talking and Little Monster was crawling around on the floor.

"Hey guys," Auntie said. "Did you have fun outside?"

"Donut please," Little Man said.

"You must be hungry," his mother said. "It's an hour later than you usually eat."

"Donut please," Cora said.

"Ok," Auntie said. "They're in the bag next to my purse by the door."

Little Man went racing over to get the donuts. But when he found the bag, it had been torn open and there was only one donut left inside.

"What happened?" he yelled. "The powdered donut is gone!"

(Powdered donuts were Little Man's favorite).

"There's nothing in here but a single glazed!" he said.

"The glazed donut is mine," Cora said.

Little Man looked around frantically. Then he saw it—a trail of white powder that streaked across the kitchen floor and led right to Little Monster.

"Hey!" Little Man cried. "Little Monster ate my donut. He has powder all over his face."

"What?" his mother said.

She walked over and picked Little Monster up off of the floor.

"Oh," she said. "He must have gotten into the bag while we were talking."

"No!" Little Man said. "I'm so hungry."

"It's ok," his mother said. "I can make you a peanut-butter sandwich or a grilled cheese."

"No!" Little Man said. "I've been waiting for a donut."

He had tears in his eyes.

"Here," Cora said.

She broke her glazed donut in two and handed half to Little Man.

"It's not a powdered donut," she said. "But half of a glazed is better than nothing."

Little Man looked at the sticky treat. He couldn't believe that Cora wanted to share. That donut was hers and she could have eaten the whole thing by herself.

"Thank you," Little Man said.

He bit into the donut. It was warm and gooey and better than he had imagined.

"See," his mother said. "Your cousin *is* like a sister to you."

"No," Little Man said. "She's better than a sister. She's a best friend."

story six

The Night Before the Championship

or

Winning Isn't Everything

THAT SUMMER WAS LITTLE Man's best season of Little League baseball. Not only did his team, The Midtown Monkeys, make it to the championship, but he had one of the highest batting averages in the league and he hit five home runs. He was even dubbed "the Little Manbino" by his teammates who said that his pudge and his power reminded them of Babe Ruth, "the Great Bambino."

Little Man loved playing sports. But because he was so clumsy, he was not a very talented athlete. He had to work extra hard in order to be good. Sometimes all of his effort paid off. It made him practice harder and take each game more seriously than many of his opponents. But sometimes it didn't. Being clumsy and trying hard can make for a bad combination—like the time he ran so fast that he tripped over first base or the time he was so focused on catching a pop fly that he didn't see his teammate and the two of them collided.

Before the season began, Little Man's father took him to the sporting goods store to buy a new glove. He picked a black one with gold trim, just like the one Ken Griffey Jr. used to wear. (Little Man learned all about Ken Griffey Jr. from his father when they took his father's old baseball card collection down from the attic and went through it together).

"The most important thing about getting a new glove," his father said, "is making sure you break it in."

That night his father showed him how to oil the glove. He put a baseball in its webbing, wrapped a rubber band around it, and put it under Little Man's mattress.

"Sleep on it tonight," his father said, "and every night this week. Then we'll take the rubber band off and work on breaking it in together."

When Little Man finally took the glove out from under his bed, it was softer and easier to open and shut. But there was still a lot of work to be done. Every afternoon after school, Little Man wore the glove around the house. He kept a baseball in it which he would take out from time to time and use to pound the webbing or beat the palm of the glove until it was tender and worn. At night he would wait for his father to come home from work and then the two of them would go out into the yard and play catch until dinner. He would take the glove off at the dinner table, put it on the seat of his chair, and sit on it like a cushion. Then, after dinner was done, he would put it back on and break it in some more while watching the Red Sox on TV.

"That's going to be the best glove in town," his mother said.

"I don't want to drop a single ball this season," Little Man said. "I want to be the best third baseman there is."

"It's good to have goals," his father said. "It's good to want to be excellent at what you do. But the people who accomplish the most are often driven by more than a desire to be the best."

"What else?" Little Man said.

"If you want to be great," his father said, "start by doing what you love. Dedicate yourself to it because you *need* to do it, because you won't be happy if you don't do it."

"I love baseball," Little Man said. "It's all I think about."

"I know you do," his father said. "That passion you feel, that excitement about doing what you love, will make you care more about doing it well than about being the best. And caring about doing it well is the only way to be the best."

"I want to win," Little Man said. "And I want to hit lots of home runs."

His father smiled.

"Work hard," he said. "Play to the best of your abilities. There's happiness in that."

Little Man disagreed. All he cared about was helping the Monkeys win the championship. When he wasn't playing base-ball, he was talking about baseball. When he wasn't talking about baseball, he was thinking about baseball. When he wasn't thinking about baseball, he was sleeping and dreaming about baseball. And always about winning.

That season was unlike any other. In addition to the fact that Little Man was playing better than he had ever played before, he was part of a great team—one destined to make it to the town championship. Little Man had a lot of friends on his team. When they didn't have practice or a game to go to, they would meet at the town park and play pickup baseball until dusk. Or, if it was a really hot day, they would play wiffleball in the vacant lot next to the town pool and then go swimming, running into the water with their clothes on in order to cool off.

After every win, the Monkeys' coach would treat them to slushies at the concession stand. And on those rare occasions when they lost, he would gather everyone together in the dugout and talk about what they had done well and what they needed to do to improve.

The night before the championship, Little Man was so excited that he could not sleep. At dinner time, he barely touched his meal. His stomach was in knots.

"What's wrong, Little Man?" his mother said. "You haven't eaten."

"Nothing," Little Man said. "I'm not that hungry."

"But pizza is your favorite food," his mother said. "And you didn't have a big lunch today."

"I'm just thinking," Little Man said. "That's all."

"Thinking about what?" his mother said.

"Thinking about winning the game tomorrow," his father said.

"I don't want anything to go wrong," Little Man said. "I don't want to do anything to screw it up."

"Just do the best you can," his father said. "You can't control anything beyond that."

"Can I wear my uniform to bed?" Little Man said.

"I don't see why not," his mother said. "But why do you want to do that?"

"I don't want to wake up late and forget to put it on," Little Man said.

"But the game isn't until 2 in the afternoon," his mother said.

"Please," Little Man said. "I don't want to take any chances."

That night Little Man waited until he heard his parents go to bed. Then, when he was sure that they were fast asleep, he snuck downstairs and went straight to the basement. The basement was where he kept his baseball bag and his cleats. Inside of the bag were his glove, his sunflower seeds, his bubblegum, and his lucky bat. He pulled the short wooden bat from the bag and held it in his hands. He studied it, felt its weight, closed his eyes and tried to remember every hit of the season, every one of his five home runs. Then he kissed the barrel of the bat and imagined himself walking up to home plate in tomorrow's championship game.

"Next up, number 58, the Little Manbino," he said.

He got into his stance and pretended to dig in at the plate.

"It all comes down to this, folks. Two on. Two out. Bottom of the ninth."

He took a swing.

"Swing and a miss by the Manbino," he said. "He got fooled by that off-speed pitch."

He swung again.

"Strike two," he said. "Manbino looks shaky up there. The pressure is getting to him."

He swung a third time.

"Crack!" he said. "It's a high fly ball hit deep to left. Back at the track, the wall . . ."

Suddenly, the lights in the basement flashed on.

Little Man turned and saw his father standing in the doorway.

"Dad," he said. "I . . ."

"Home run!" his father yelled. "The Monkeys win! The Monkeys win!"

He raced over, scooped Little Man up into his arms, and the two of them jumped and danced and laughed in celebration without knowing whether tomorrow would bring victory or defeat and, for a short time, without caring either way.

story seven

A Trip to the Mountains

or

I Ain't Afraid of No Ghosts

AFTER BASEBALL SEASON HAD come to an end, it was time for Little Man and his family to go on vacation. Every summer they spent one week in the mountains at a cabin on a lake and the next week by the shore at the beach. The cabin they stayed at had once belonged to Little Man's great grandparents (his mother's grandparents) and he could still remember Great Gram talking fondly about her summers at the lake house.

When he used to visit Great Gram, Little Man would sit on her lap and she would give him candy and sweets and then let him march around the room pushing her walker as if it was his. She had lived in a small apartment down the street with her cat Mitzy. Mitzy was a messy cat, always tearing up furniture, knocking things on the floor, and making stains on the carpet. She even stole Great Gram's glasses right off of the nightstand and was found playing with them under the bed. But in spite of the fact that she could be a handful, Mitzy was a sweet cat and Great Gram loved her. She gave Mitzy plenty of treats (maybe too many!), always fed her a little people-food off of her plate, and even let Mitzy sleep next to her on her pillow.

"She rules the roost," Great Gram would say. "I'm just her guest in this apartment."

When Great Gram died, Little Man was very sad. He didn't understand why he couldn't see her any more.

"Death is a sad thing," his mother said. "No one should act like it isn't. But we also believe that we'll see Great Gram again. We hope for that with all of our hearts."

"How can we know for sure?" Little Man said.

"We *hope*," his mother said. "And hope has more to do with loving than with knowing."

"I love Great Gram," Little Man said. "I miss her."

"I know you do," his mother said. "So do I. But as long as we live, our love will live too. It will never leave us."

It was a five hour drive north to the family cabin. The trip took them through the woods, over the mountains, and around the lake. For half of the drive, Little Man napped; long trips made him sleepy and as soon as he closed his eyes, he was out cold. For the other half, he listened to Little Monster babble and sing. Little Monster was getting bigger now. He was able to crawl and to stand and he could communicate by pointing his finger at whatever he wanted and making noises like "goo" and "dah."

Little Man had grown very fond of his little brother. In fact, they had become best friends. Little Monster followed Little Man from room to room and tried to imitate everything he did. He even had his own tiny baseball glove which he loved to wear, just like his big brother.

"Someday I'll teach you how to play catch," Little Man said. "You won't be as good as me, but you'll still be pretty good and we can be on the same team and we'll win every game."

"Ya, ya!" Little Monster yelled.

(That was his favorite saying).

"I'll play third base and you can be the shortstop."

"Ya, ya!" Little Monster yelled.

"Ok," Little Man said. "It's a deal."

When they finally arrived at the cabin, Little Man was so sick of being cooped up in the car that he ran straight down to the water and dove in, clothes and all. The water was crisp. Cold and clear. He dunked his head and heard nothing but the silence of the lake, felt the water ripple around him. Then he emerged and began splashing and playing.

"Little Man!" his father called.

He was standing on the shoreline.

"Now your shoes are all wet!"

"It's fun," Little Man said. "Come on in!"

"Not now," his father said. "Come help us carry our bags in from the car."

Little Man dunked his head once more. He closed his eyes and thought of Great Gram. How many times had she looked out at this very lake from the shore? Then he swam back and walked up the lawn to the car, his shoes squeaking the whole way.

The week at the cabin was so much fun. Little Man went hiking and fishing, kayaking and swimming in the lake. At night he would lie out on the grass and look up at the stars. It was hard to believe that there could be so many. The sky seemed clearer in the mountains. The planets and the stars were so easy to see and Little Man loved lying on his back and looking straight up into the heavens.

"How many stars are there?" he said.

"I don't know," his father said. "Probably more than anyone could count."

"How did they get there?" Little Man said.

"That's a mystery," his father said. "It's something that every philosopher and scientist and little boy has wondered."

"Hey!" Little Man said. "Who are you calling a *little boy*?"

His father laughed.

"We're all little," he said. "We like to pretend that we aren't. But when I look up at the night sky, I remember just how little I am."

"But little things are important too," Little Man said.

"Of course," his father said. "Sometimes the littlest things are the most important."

"Like Little Monster?" Little Man said.

"Yes," his father said. "Like every little man and little monster who has ever walked this earth."

Little Man smiled.

"Come on," his father said. "Let's go build a campfire and roast some marshmallows."

"Yum," Little Man said. "Can we make s'mores?"

"Sure," his father said. "As long as your mother hasn't eaten all of the chocolate."

The fire crackled and hissed and Little Man listened to the crickets singing in the trees. He ate s'more after s'more until his belly was good and full. Then he laid his head on his father's shoulder and fell sound asleep.

The next day, Little Man's aunt and uncle joined them at the cabin and they brought their dog Marty with them. Marty was a funny puppy, playful and skittish. He acted like he was brave, barking at squirrels and chasing chipmunks around the yard; but in reality he was a scaredy dog, afraid to go in the water and frightened by the sound of thunder.

Little Man loved Marty. They would spend hours playing fetch with a tennis ball and every morning Little Man would save his bacon from breakfast and use it to get Marty to do tricks. He taught Marty to sit and to stay and roll over and he hid his extra bacon under his bed where no one could find it.

"He's very good with dogs," his uncle said to his father. "You should think about getting him one of his own."

"I want to get him a dog," his father said. "But I have to convince his mother first."

"Just come home with one," his uncle said. "She can't say 'No' once it's in the house."

Little Man's father considered this. (He secretly wanted a dog. He had wanted one his whole life). But he didn't say anything and he didn't mention it again.

That night they built another campfire and Little Man's uncle thought it would be a good idea to tell ghost stories. Little Man didn't like ghost stories. They always scared him and he did not like feeling afraid. But he didn't want to seem like a chicken either. He wanted to be a brave little man, not a little baby.

"I ain't afraid of no ghosts," he told his uncle.

"Good," his uncle said. "Then I'll tell you a story about this very cabin!"

Little Man became uneasy. He didn't want to hear that the place where he was staying tonight might be haunted.

As his uncle told the tale of how the cabin had once been part of a fancy resort—that is, until the resort burned down in a great fire—Little Man began to tremble.

Yelp! Yelp! The sound of Marty barking came loudly from the house.

"I can't imagine what's gotten into him," Little Man's uncle said.

"Something must have scared him," his aunt said.

"Maybe it's a ghost!" Little Man said.

His uncle laughed.

"No," he said. "This place isn't haunted. It was just a story, Little Man. Come on. We'll go check on Marty together."

"I don't know . . ." Little Man said. "You check. Maybe I'll sleep out here tonight."

"Come on," his uncle said. "I'm sure that all Marty needs is a little bit of comfort from his favorite little man."

"Ok," Little Man said. "But you go first."

When they entered the cabin, Marty was nowhere to be found.

"That's strange," his uncle said. "I know he's in here. I just heard him."

Little Man was frightened. He began to tremble.

"Maybe a ghost got him!" he said.

"Don't worry, Little Man," his uncle said. "There's no such thing as ghosts."

Yelp! Suddenly, a strange white figure came rushing toward them at full speed.

"Ah!" Little Man cried. "A ghost! A ghost!"

The figure leaped through the air and tackled Little Man to the ground.

"Eek!" he yelled. "It's got me! It's trying to drag me away! Help! Help!"

The ghost started barking and wagging its tale and soon it was licking Little Man's face with its big wet tongue.

"That's no ghost," Little Man's uncle said. "That's Marty. He got himself wrapped up in a bedsheet. That's all."

His uncle pulled the sheet off of the dog.

It was Marty after all!

"Phew!" Little Man said. "I was so scared."

"I wonder what he was doing in the bedroom," his uncle said. "He usually doesn't go in there."

"I think I know," Little Man said.

He took his uncle to the bedroom and showed him the secret stash of bacon hidden under his bed.

"That's what he was after!" his uncle said. "See, there's nothing to be afraid of. Just a hungry dog."

"I'm glad," Little Man said. "But I'm still feeling a little scared. Do you think Marty can sleep in here with me tonight? Just for some extra protection?"

"Sure," his uncle said. "But I don't know how good of a guard dog he'll be. He's about as wimpy as they come."

"That makes the two of us," Little Man said and he patted Marty on the head. "We can protect each other."

When the week was over, Little Man was sad to go. He had had so much fun in mountains and he wouldn't be back for a whole year. But he was also excited to get to the shore house and to spend some time at the beach. He helped his parents pack the car, said goodbye to his aunt and uncle, gave the rest of the bacon he had been saving to Marty, and said a silent prayer to Great Gram thanking her for letting him use the house she loved so much.

Then he got into the car.

"It's going to be a long ride," he said to Little Monster. "No whining. Close your eyes and we'll be at the beach before you know it."

story eight

The Cape Cod Classic

or

Winning Isn't Everything, Dad

LITTLE MAN'S NANA AND Papa owned a house by the beach and his father had been vacationing there ever since he was a little boy. That meant that everywhere they went, he insisted on telling *boring dad stories*. Boring dad stories usually began with the words "When I was a boy . . ." and went on to recount a memory from Little Man's father's childhood. Here are some examples:

"When I was a boy, that house was a gift shop called *Thelma's* and your crazy uncle and I would save up our allowances in order to buy cap guns and baseball cards."

"When I was a boy, that ice cream shop was called *The Smuggler* and they made homemade ice cream, the best anyone had ever tasted."

"When I was a boy, we needed one more person to play wiffleball at the beach but our friend Santino went fishing instead."

"When I was a boy blah, blah, blah, blah, blah . . ."

Little Man didn't mind his father's stories—he actually kind of liked them—but his mother had heard enough.

"Do you know how many times you've told us about that gift shop?" she said.

"I don't know," his father said. "Four or five?"

"More like four or five hundred!" she said.

Everyone laughed.

"Oh no," Little Man's father said. "I'm becoming just like my dad. Papa tells the same boring stories over and over again too!"

"Your stories aren't so bad," Little Man said. "Little Monster, do you think dad's stories are boring?"

"Ya, ya!" Little Monster said.

Everyone laughed again.

Little Man's father was sentimental. But his Papa was even more so. In the cellar of the beach house, Papa had a secret box full of treasures: keys and coins and trinkets that he had been collecting all his life. He liked to keep things that reminded him of important moments, things that brought him back to his childhood or to a special day in the past.

"Little Man," he said one afternoon when everyone was getting ready for the beach. "Come to the basement. I have something I want to show you."

Little Man followed Papa downstairs.

"Over here," Papa said. "By the tool chest."

"What's that?" Little Man said.

Papa took a box down from the top shelf and opened it.

"These," he said, "are some of my most prized possessions. I keep a lot of special things in this box."

"What's that?" Little Man said pointing in the box.

"This was my grandfather's cigar case," Papa said. "And this was his favorite tie pin."

"Wow," Little Man said. "They look so old."

"They are old," Papa said. "They belonged to your great, great grandfather."

Papa showed him every item in the box; some he had been saving since he was as little as Little Man. Each had a story behind it, a memory that made it special, that filled it with meaning.

"What's this?" Little Man asked.

"That's a penny I found in the parking lot at the hospital on the day you were born."

"And what's this?"

"That's my seat card from your parents' wedding."

"And this?"

"That's the stamp that was on the first letter your Nana sent me when we started dating."

Little Man loved looking through Papa's treasure box. He loved hearing stories from long ago and learning things that Papa told nobody but him.

At the bottom of the box was a bright pink golf ball. Little Man reached in and pulled it out. He didn't have to ask what it was. He already knew.

"There she is," Papa said. "My lucky ball."

Every summer, all of Little Man's cousins would get together at Nana and Papa's beach house and the guys would go minigolfing while the girls had a night to themselves. It was an annual tradition: The Cape Cod Classic. The most competitive, cut-throat game of mini-golf there was. The stakes were high. Real high. The winner got his name engraved on The Cape Cod Classic trophy. The player with worst score had to buy ice cream for everyone.

Papa was the reigning champ. He had won the Classic more times than anyone else. And he attributed all of his success to his lucky pink ball.

"Is it true," Little Man said, "that you used this ball in the very first Classic?"

"The first Classic," Papa said. "Which was also my first win."

"When was that?" Little Man said.

"Oh," Papa said. "That was years and years ago. Back when your father was even littler than you. Back when his Papa, my father, played with us."

"And you've been using it ever since?"

"Ole Pinky?" Papa said. "She's served me well all these years."

"Will you use it this year?" Little Man said.

"No," Papa said. "Not me. You."

"Me?" Little Man said.

"You," Papa said.

"But I'll never win," Little Man said.

"I don't know," Papa said. "I have a feeling that this may be your year. And even if it's not, as long as your father doesn't win, I'll be happy. He's never won the Classic. Not once in all these years. We can't let him start now."

"He's been practicing," Little Man said. "He took me and Little Monster just last week."

"That's ok," Papa said. "We have a secret weapon. Ole Pinky. Our lucky ball."

Little Man smiled.

"Don't tell anyone I gave her to you," Papa said. "Not until the night of the big game."

"I won't," Little Man said. "It'll be our secret."

Little Man spent the afternoon with his family at the beach. He built sandcastles and let Little Monster knock them down, he caught hermit crabs and chased seagulls into the water, he collected sea glass, went swimming, and played a game of tag football with his father and his crazy uncle. But the whole time, all he could think about was The Cape Cod Classic. Would Ole Pinky bring him luck? Was this really his year? Would he taste the sweetness of victory before his father ever did?

"What's on your mind, Little Man?" Nana said.

"Nothing," Little Man said. "Just thinking, that's all."

"What are you thinking about?" Nana said. "And what were you doing earlier in the cellar with Papa?"

"Huh?" Little Man said. "The cellar? When?"

"Before the beach," Nana said. "You were down there for quite some time."

Little Man looked at Papa.

Papa winked.

"Oh we were just . . . fixing the lawnmower," Little Man said.

"Fixing the lawnmower?" Nana said.

"That's right," Papa said. "One of the blades was loose."

Nana gave them a skeptical look.

"Yup," Little Man said. "What else would we be doing in a musty old cellar?"

The night before the Classic, Little Man slept with the pink golf ball under his pillow. He wanted to soak up as much luck as he possibly could. He closed his eyes and imagined seeing his name engraved next to Papa's on the trophy. He fell fast asleep and before he knew it, it was morning: the day of The Cape Cod Classic.

"I hate to say it," his father said at breakfast. "But I'm feeling pretty good about my chances."

"You feel pretty good every year," his crazy uncle said. "And it always ends the same."

"We'll see," his father said.

"We will see," his cousin Noah said. "I've been practicing in my dorm. My roommate brought his putter to school and I've been shooting at a solo cup for weeks."

"Now that I work the day shift," his uncle Rock said, "I'm not as tired as I was in years past. I'm rested and ready to go."

"You're all sunk," Papa said.

"What are you talking about?" Little Man's father said.

"Go on Little Man," Papa said. "Show them."

Little Man took the pink ball from his pocket.

"Is that Ole Pinky?" his crazy uncle said.

Little Man nodded.

"That's not fair," his father said. "You never let me use Ole Pinky and I asked every year when I was a kid."

"Tough luck, son," Papa said. "She belongs to Little Man now."

Little Man smiled.

"I don't like it," his father said. "I don't like it one bit."

It was a grueling game of mini-golf, back and forth the entire day. But as they approached the 18th hole, Little Man's father and his Papa were tied for the lead.

Papa shot first and he hit a beauty. It rolled down the slope, through the windmill, over the rough, and ended up less than a foot from the hole.

"Good luck following that one," he said to Little Man's father.

His father gave Papa a dirty look.

"I mean it," Papa said. "I wouldn't want you to choke here on the 18th green. It would haunt you for the rest of your life."

Little Man's father stepped up to the tee, closed his eyes, took a deep breath, and swung.

The ball spun slowly down the slope.

Everyone was still.

It rolled through the windmill.

No one said a word.

It rolled over the rough.

Silence.

It hit the hole and spun around and around the rim.

"No!" Papa yelled.

"Yes!" Little Man's father yelled.

He had sunk the shot.

A hole in one.

"It's over!" he said. "I won! I won!"

He was jumping up and down like happy child.

"Not so fast," Papa said. "The others still have to shoot."

When Little Man stepped up to the tee, his heart was pounding in his chest. He knew that he couldn't win. But if he managed to knock Papa's ball in the hole, that would force a tie between Papa and his father. They would need to play a one hole playoff to decide who was the champ. Little Man kissed Ole Pinky before placing it on the tee. Then he closed his eyes, took a deep breath, and swung.

"No!" his father yelled.

"Yes!" Papa cheered. "You did it Little Man! You did it! It's not over yet!"

Little Man had knocked Papa's ball clean into the hole. Ole Pinky had come through again. Her luck hadn't run out.

Before Papa or Little Man's father had reached the playoff hole, Little Man stopped them.

"Wait," he said. "Here Papa, I think you should use Ole Pinky on this one—just for luck."

"Not fair!" his father said. "No switching balls mid-Classic!"

"Just do the best you can," Little Man said. "Work hard and play to the best of your abilities. There's happiness in that."

His father rolled his eyes and walked over to the green.

And even before they shot, everyone knew who the winner would be.

epilogue

Happy Birthday Little Man

or

Two Surprises are Better than One

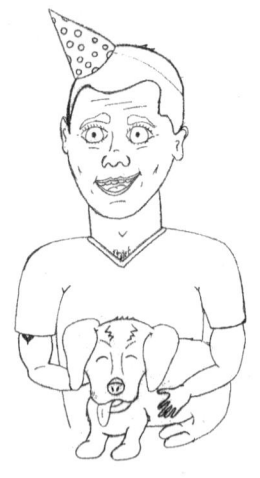

IT WAS A COOL autumn day in October and Little Man was excited. It was his birthday. Most years Little Man's birthday fell on a weekday, but not this year. This year his birthday was on Sunday and that meant that Little Man could spend the day doing one of his favorite fall activities: watching football.

So far it had been a perfect weekend. On the Friday before his birthday, Little Man had brought cupcakes to school and shared them with the whole class. That night his football team, the Mighty Mites, had won the toughest game of the season against their long-time rival, the Shrewsbury Shrimps. They won in double overtime and Little Man had made an important block on the game winning drive. On Saturday, his parents hosted a party for him and all of his friends. The boys played capture the flag in the backyard until dark and then they came in and ate cake and ice cream. Everyone sang "Happy Birthday" to Little Man and even Little Monster clapped and tried to sing along.

Today promised to be a good day as well. It was Little Man's birthday and his whole family was coming over to watch football and to eat more cake and ice cream. Everyone was going to be there: Nana and Papa, his crazy uncle, Auntie and Cora, all of his cousins, Pup Paul and Beow, his godmother Katie and her brother Soup, even Marty who he hadn't seen since the summer.

Little Man was so excited that he could hardly contain himself.

"This is going to be the best birthday ever!" he announced.

"It is," his father said. "And when everyone gets here, I have a special birthday surprise."

"You do?" Little Man said.

"I do," his father said.

Little Man could not wait. He wanted to know the surprise right now. But his father refused to tell him.

"A surprise is only a surprise if you don't know what it is," he said. "You'll find out soon enough."

As his parents decorated the house and got things ready for their guests, Little Man's curiosity grew and grew. He decided to snoop around to see what he could find. He pretended that he was a spy who had gone undercover and was searching a villain's secret lair for clues. He was upstairs rummaging through his parents' bedroom draws when his mother's cellphone began to ring.

Little Man walked over and picked it up off of her dresser.

"A top secret phone call," he said. "Good thing we tapped the wires."

He was going to bring the phone downstairs to his mother but accidently pressed a button on the side and answered it instead.

"Hello?" said the voice on the other end. "Hello?"

"Hello?" Little Man said.

"This is Dr. Brenda," the voice said. "I have some very good news."

The doctor thought Little Man was his mother. He was a little upset to know that his voice could be confused with a woman's, but he listened carefully all the same.

Later that afternoon, when everyone had arrived, Little Man's father gathered them together in the living room.

"I have a surprise!" he said.

"Make it quick," Pup Paul said. "Kickoff is only 5 minutes away!"

"I already know the surprise!" Little Man said.

"You do?" his father said.

"Yes," Little Man said. "Mom is having another baby. And this time it's a girl, a little princess for me to play with and protect!"

"What?" his father said.

He was shocked.

"I . . . I didn't want to say anything until I knew for sure," his mother said.

"What?!?" his father said.

Everyone was excited.

There was laughter and cheering and commotion.

"How could you not tell me?" his father said.

"Wait a second," Little Man said. "If that wasn't your surprise, what was it?"

Just then Little Man's crazy uncle walked in from the other room. He was holding a puppy in his arms, a little golden retriever which was barking and wagging its tail.

Happy Birthday Little Man or Two Surprises are Better than One

"What?!" Little Man's mother said.

"I wanted it to be a surprise for *everyone*," his father said.

"What?!?" Little Man's mother said. "How could you not tell me?"

"I guess the house is going to be a little crowded after all," Little Man said.

He took his new puppy into his arms and hugged it with all of his might.

The End.